Riot at M

from A Suitable Boy

VIKRAM SETH

A Phoenix Paperback

A Suitable Boy first published in Great Britain
in 1993 by Phoenix House
A paperback edition published in 1994 by Phoenix

This extract consisting of part 15.10 to 15.21 of *A Suitable Boy* first
published in Great Britain in 1996 by Phoenix
A Division of Orion Books Ltd
Orion House, 5 Upper St Martin's Lane, London WC2H 9EA

A CIP catalogue record for this book is available
from the British Library.

ISBN: 1 85799 599 6

Typeset by Datix International Ltd, Bungay, Suffolk
Printed in Great Britain by Clays Ltd, St Ives plc

The Bharat Milaap processions began on time. Since Bharat had merely to go to the outskirts of his city to meet his brother, he bided his time until the pandit gave him the signal; but Rama had a long journey to make to the holy capital of Ayodhya – to which he was returning in triumph after many years of exile – and just as it became dark he set out on this journey from a temple situated a good half-mile away from the stage where the brothers were at last to be united.

This stage had been festooned with strings of flowers suspended from the bamboo poles that rose from its four corners; it had been put together by almost the whole neighbourhood with much advice and many marigolds; and several cows that had attempted to eat the marigolds had been shooed off by the monkey army. The cows were normally welcome enough in the neighbourhood – their movements at least were unobstructed – and the poor trusting things must have wondered what had created such a sudden change in their popularity.

Today was a day of pure joy and celebration; for not only were Rama and Lakshman to be reunited with their brothers Bharat and Shatrughan, but it was the day when the people would see their Lord return to them, to rule over them and establish perfect righteousness not only in

Ayodhya but in the entire world.

The procession began to wind its way through the narrow lanes of Misri Mandi to the sound of drums and shehnais and a raucous popular band. First came the lights, courtesy of Jawaharlal Light House, the same company that had provided the demons' red eyes the previous evening. The brilliant lights they held above them emitted an intense white glow from what looked like bulbs covered with gauze cloth.

Mahesh Kapoor held his hand against his eyes. He was here partly because his wife wanted him to be, partly because he was more and more coming around to the idea of rejoining the Congress Party and felt he should re-establish his links with his old constituency just in case.

'This light is too bright – I'm going blind –' he said. 'Kedarnath, do something about it. You're one of the organizers, aren't you?'

'Baoji, let's just let them pass. It'll be better later on,' said his son-in-law, who knew that once the procession had begun, there was almost nothing he could do about it. Mrs Mahesh Kapoor had cupped her hands over her ears, but was smiling to herself.

The brass band was deafening. After blaring out a few film songs, they switched to religious melodies. They made a striking sight in their cheap red trousers with white piping and their blue tunics with gold-coloured cotton braid. Every one of their trumpets, trombones and horns was out of tune.

2

Then came the principal noisemongers, the flat drummers, who had been roasting their instruments carefully over three small fires near the temple to heighten their pitch and crispness. They played as if they had gone mad – in unbelievably swift salvos of unbearable noise. They forced themselves aggressively upon anyone whom they recognized from the Ramlila Committee in a mixture of display and blackmail, compelling them to hand over coins and notes. They thrust their pelvises forward and moved their drums back and forth at a slant from their waists. These were good days for the drummers: they were in demand both by those who celebrated Dussehra and by those who observed Moharram.

'Where are they from?' asked Mahesh Kapoor.

'What?' asked Kedarnath.

'I said, where are they from?'

'I can't hear you because of these wretched drummers.'

Mahesh Kapoor cupped his hands and shouted into his son-in-law's ears: 'I said, where are they from? Are they Muslim?'

'They're from the market –' shouted Kedarnath, which was a way of admitting that they were.

Even before the swaroops – Rama, Lakshman, and Sita – could appear in their beauty and glory, the master of fireworks – who carried a massive sack on his shoulder – brought out a huge packet, tore off the coloured paper from it, ripped open the cardboard box inside, and rolled out another great red carpet of five thousand firecrackers. 3

As they exploded in series, people drew back from the light and noise, their faces flushed with excitement, their hands clapped over their ears or their fingers inserted into them. The noise was so overwhelming that Mahesh Kapoor decided that even his obligation to be seen in his old constituency was not worth the loss of his hearing and sanity.

'Come,' he shouted to his wife, 'we're going home.'

Mrs Mahesh Kapoor could not hear a word of what he was saying, and kept smiling.

The monkey army, Bhaskar included, was next in the procession, and a great quiver of excitement went through the spectators; the swaroops were to follow shortly. The children started clapping; the old people were the most expectant of all, remembering perhaps the scores of Ramlilas they must have seen enacted in the course of their lives. Some children sat on a low wall along the route, others skilfully scrambled up to the ledges of houses, getting a foothold here or the help of an adult shoulder there. One father, kissing his two-year-old daughter's bare foot, pushed her up onto the flat top of a decorative pillar and held her there to help her get a better view.

And then at last Lord Rama appeared; and Sita, in a yellow sari; and Lakshman, smiling, his quiver glistening with arrows.

The eyes of the spectators filled with tears of joy, and they began showering flowers on the swaroops. The children clambered down from their perches and followed the procession, chanting 'Jai Siyaram' and 'Ramchandra ji ki jai!' and sprinkling rose-petals and water from the Ganga on them. And the drummers beat their drums with renewed frenzy.

Mahesh Kapoor, his face flushed with annoyance, seized his wife's hand and pulled her to one side.

'We are leaving,' he shouted directly into her ear. 'Can't you hear me? I have had enough.... Veena, your mother and I are leaving.'

Mrs Mahesh Kapoor looked at her husband, astonished, almost disbelieving. Tears filled her eyes when she understood what he had said, what she was to be deprived of. Once she had seen the Bharat Milaap at Nati Imli in Banaras, and she had never forgotten it. The tenderness of the occasion – with the two brothers who had remained in Ayodhya throwing themselves at the feet of their two long-exiled brothers – the throng of spectators, at least a lakh of people – the devotion in everyone's eyes as the small figures came onto the stage – everything came back to her. Whenever she saw the Bharat Milaap here in Brahmpur she thought of that occasion in all its charm and wonder and grace. How simple it was and how wonderful. And it was not merely the tender meeting of long-separated brothers but the first act of Ram Rajya, the rule of Rama when, unlike in these factious, violent, petty times, the four pillars of religion – truth, purity, mercy, and charity – would hold up the edifice of the world.

5

The words of Tulsidas, long known by heart, came back to her:

> Devoted to duty, the people walked in the path of the Vedas, each according to his own caste and stage of life, and enjoyed perfect happiness, unvexed by fear, or sorrow, or disease.

'Let us at least wait till the procession has reached Ayodhya,' Mrs Mahesh Kapoor pleaded with her husband.

'Stay if you want. I'm going,' snapped Mahesh Kapoor; and, forlornly, she followed. But she decided that tomorrow she would not persuade him to come for Rama's coronation. She would come alone and, not subject to his whims and commands, she would see it from beginning to end. She would not be prised away yet again from a scene that her soul thirsted for.

Meanwhile the procession wound its way through the labyrinthine alleys of Misri Mandi and the contiguous neighbourhoods. Lakshman stepped on one of the burnt-out bulbs from the Jawaharlal Light House, and yelped in pain. Since there was no water to be had immediately, Rama picked up some rose-petals that had been strewn in his path and crushed them against the burn. The people sighed at this sign of brotherly solicitude, and the procession moved on. The chief of fireworks now set off a few green-flared rockets that soared into the sky before exploding in a chrysanthemum of sparks. At this, Hanuman rushed forward, waving his tail, as if reminded of his own incendiary activities in Lanka. He was followed by the monkey throng, chattering and shouting with joy; they reached the marigold stage a couple of hundred yards before the three main swaroops. Hanuman, who today was even redder, plumper and jollier than he had been yesterday, leaped onto the stage, hopped, skipped, and danced for a few seconds, then jumped off. Now Bharat understood that Rama and Lakshman were approaching the river Saryu and the city of Ayodhya, and he too began to move towards the stage along the lane from the other side.

2

And then suddenly Rama's procession stopped, and the sound of other drums was heard together with cries of terrible grief and lamentation. A group of about twenty men accompanied by drummers was trying to cut across the procession in order to get to the Imambara with their tazia. Some were beating their breasts in sorrow for Imam Hussain; in the hands of others were chains and whips tipped with small knives and razor-blades with which they lashed themselves mercilessly in jerky, compulsive motions. They were an hour-and-a-half behind time – their drummers had turned up late, they had got into a scuffle with another tazia procession – and now they were trying to push forward as fast as they could, desperate to get to their destination. It was the ninth night of Moharram. In the distance they could just make out the spire of the Imambara lit up with a string of lights. They moved forwards, tears coursing down their cheeks –

'Ya Hassan! Ya Hussain!' 'Ya Hassan! Ya Hussain!' 'Hassan! Hussain!' 'Hassan! Hussain!'

'Bhaskar,' said Veena to her son, who had grabbed her hand – 'Go home at once. At once. Where's Daadi? –'

'But I want to watch –'

She slapped him once, hard, across his monkey-face. He looked at her unbelievingly, then, crying, backed out of the lane.

Kedarnath had moved forward to talk to the two policemen accompanying the tazia procession. Not caring what her neighbours might think, she went up to him, caught his hands in her own, and said:

'Let's go home.'

'But there's trouble here – I'd better –'

'Bhaskar's ill.'

Kedarnath, torn between two anxieties, nodded.

The two policemen accompanying the tazia-bearers tried to clear a path for them, but this was too much for the people of Misri Mandi, the citizens of the holy city of Ayodhya who had waited so long and devotedly for a sight of Lord Rama.

The policemen realized that what would have been a safe path an hour previously was no longer safe. They ordered, then pleaded with the tazia procession to change its route, to halt, to go back, but to no avail. The desperate mourners thrust forward through the joyous celebrators.

This atrocious and violent interruption – this lunatic mourning that made a mockery of the enactment of Shri Ramachandra ji returning to his home, his brothers, his people, to establish his perfect reign – was not to be borne. The monkeys, who had just been leaping about in uncontrollable joy, angrily threw flowers onto the tazia, shouted and growled aggressively, and then stood threateningly around the intruders who were attempting to force themselves across the path of Rama, Sita and Lakshman.

The actor playing Rama himself moved forward in a motion that was half aggressive, half propitiatory.

A chain lashed out, and he staggered back, to lie gasping in pain against the ledge of a shop. Upon his dark blue skin a red stain formed and spread.

The crowd went berserk. What all the forces of Ravana had not succeeded in doing these bloodthirsty Muslims had managed to do. It was not a young actor, but God himself who lay wounded there.

Crazed by the sight of the wounded Rama, the man with the fireworks seized a lathi from one of the organizers and led the crowd in a charge against the tazia procession. Within seconds, the tazia, many weeks' work of delicate glass and mica and paper tracery, lay smashed on the ground. Fireworks were thrown onto it and it was set alight. The maddened crowd stamped on it and beat it with lathis until it was charred and splintered. Its horrified defenders slashed out with their knives and chains at these kafirs, leaping about like apes on the very eve of the great martyrdom, who had dared to desecrate the holy image of the tomb.

The sight of the crushed and blackened tazia made them mad.

Both sides now were filled with the lust to kill – what did it matter if they too suffered martyrdom? – to attack pure evil, to defend what was dear to them – what did it matter if they died? – whether to recreate the passion of Karbala or to re-establish Ram Rajya and rid the world of the murderous, cow-slaughtering, God-defiling devils.

'Kill the bastards – finish them off – the spawn of Pakistan –'

'Ya Hussain! Ya Hussain!' It was now a battlecry.

Soon even the crazed cries of the time of Partition – 'Allah-u-Akbar' and 'Har har Mahadeva' – were heard above the screams of pain and terror. Knives and spears and axes and lathis had appeared from the neighbouring houses, and Hindus and Muslims hacked at each other's limbs, eyes, faces, guts, throats. Of the two policemen, one was wounded in the back, the other managed to escape. But it was a Hindu neighbourhood and, after a few terrifying minutes of mutual butchery, the Muslims fled down side-lanes, most of them small and unfamiliar. Some were hunted down and killed, some escaped and rushed back in the direction from which they had come, some ran forward towards the Imambara by circuitous routes – guided from far off by its illuminated spire and festoons of light. They fled towards the Imambara as one would flee towards a sanctuary – where they would receive protection among those of their own religion and would find hearts that could understand their own fear and hatred and bitterness and grief – for they had seen their friends and relatives killed and wounded – and be inflamed by them in turn.

Soon Muslim mobs would be roaming around other parts of Brahmpur setting fire to Hindu shops and murdering any Hindu they could find. Meanwhile in Misri Mandi, three of the Muslim drummers who had been hired for the Bharat Milaap, who were not even Shias, and who did not care much more for the tazias than they did for the divinity of Rama, lay murdered by the wall of the temple, their drums smashed in, their heads half hacked off, their bodies doused in kerosene and set alight – all, doubtless, to the greater glory of God.

3

Maan and Firoz were sauntering along through the dark lane of Katra Mast towards Misri Mandi when Maan stopped suddenly. The sounds he heard approaching them were not those he had expected. They were the sounds neither of a tazia procession – and surely it was too late for a tazia procession – nor the joyful sounds of Bharat Milaap. The sound of drums had stopped on either side – and neither 'Hassan! Hussain!' nor 'Jai Siyaram!' could be heard. Instead he made out the ominous, inchoate sounds of a mob, broken by screams of pain or passion – or shouts of 'Har har Mahadeva'. This aggressive invocation of Shiva would not have sounded out of place yesterday – but today it chilled his blood.

He let go of Firoz's hand and turned him around by the shoulders. 'Run!' he said, his mouth dry with fear. 'Run.' His heart was pounding. Firoz stared at him but did not move.

The crowd was rushing down the lane now. The sounds grew closer. Maan looked around him in desperation. The shops were all closed, their shutters down. There were no side-lanes within immediate reach.

'Get back, Firoz –' said Maan, trembling. 'Get back – run! There's nowhere to hide here –'

'What's the matter – isn't it the procession?' Firoz's mouth opened as he registered the terror in Maan's eyes.

'Just listen to me,' Maan gasped – 'Do as I say. Run back! Run back towards the Imambara. I'll delay them for a minute or two. That'll be enough. They'll stop me first.'

'I'm not leaving you,' said Firoz.

'Firoz, you fool, this is a Hindu mob. I'm not in danger. But I won't be all right if I come with you. God knows what will be happening there by now. If there's rioting going on, they'll be killing Hindus there.'

'No –'

'Oh God –'

By now the crowd had almost reached them, and it was too late to flee. Ahead of the pack was a young man, who looked as if he was drunk. His kurta was torn and he was bleeding from a cut along his ribs. He had a blood-stained lathi in his hand, and he made for Maan and Firoz. Behind him – though it was dark and difficult to see – must have been some twenty or thirty men, armed with spears and knives or flaming torches doused in kerosene.

'Mussalmans – kill them also –'

'We're not Mussalmans,' said Maan immediately, not looking at Firoz. He tried to control his voice, but it was high-pitched with terror.

'We can find that out quickly enough,' said the young man nastily. Maan looked at him – he had a lean, clean-shaven face – a handsome face, but one that was full of madness and rage and hatred. Who was he? Who were these people? Maan recognized none of them in the darkness. What had happened? How had the peacefulness of the Bharat Milaap suddenly turned into a riot? And what, he thought, his brain seizing up with fear, what was going to happen?

Suddenly, as if by a miracle, the fog of fear dispersed from his mind.

'No need to find out who we are,' he said in a deeper voice. 'We were frightened because we thought at first you might be Muslims. We couldn't hear what you were shouting.'

'Recite the Gayatri Mantra,' sneered the young man.

Maan promptly recited the few sacred syllables. 'Now go –' he said. 'Don't threaten innocent people. Be on your way. Jai Siyaram! Har har Mahadeva!' He could not keep the rising mockery out of his voice.

The young man hesitated.

Someone in the crowd cried: 'The other's a Muslim. Why would he be dressed like that?'

'Yes, that's certain.'

'Take off his fancy dress.'

Firoz had started trembling again. This encouraged them.

'See if he's circumcized.'

'Kill the cruel, cow-murdering haramzada – cut the sister-fucker's throat.'

'What are you?' said the young man, prodding Firoz in the stomach with his bloodstained lathi. 'Quick – speak – speak, before I use this on your head –'

Firoz flinched and trembled. The blood on the lathi had stained his white sherwani. He did not lack courage normally, but now – in the face of such wild, unreasoning danger – he found he had lost his voice. How could he argue with a mob? He swallowed and said: 'I am what I am. What's that to you?'

14

Maan was looking desperately around him. He knew there was no time to talk. Suddenly in the erratic, terrifying light of the blazing torches his eyes fell on someone he thought he recognized.

'Nand Kishor!' he shouted. 'What are you doing here in this gang? Aren't you ashamed of yourself? You're supposed to be a teacher.' Nand Kishor, a middle-aged, bespectacled man, looked sullen.

'Shut up –' said the young man to Maan viciously. 'Just because you like circumcized cocks do you think we'll let the Mussalman go?' Again he prodded Firoz and drew another smear of blood down his sherwani.

Maan ignored him and continued to address Nand Kishor. He knew that the time for dialogue was short. It was miraculous that they had been able to speak at all – that they were still alive.

'You teach my nephew Bhaskar. He's part of Hanuman's army. Do you teach him to attack innocent people? Is this the kind of Ram Rajya you want to bring about? We're doing no one any harm. Let us go on our way. Come!' he said to Firoz, grabbing him by the shoulder. 'Come.' He tried to shoulder his way past the mob.

'Not so fast. You can go, you sister-fucking traitor – but you can't,' said the young man.

Maan turned on him and, ignoring his lathi, caught him by the throat in sudden fury.

'You mother-fucker!' he said to him in a low growl 15

that nevertheless carried to every man in the mob. 'Do you know what day this is? This man is my brother, more than my brother, and today in our neighbourhood we were celebrating Bharat Milaap. If you harm one hair of my brother's head – if even one hair of his head is harmed – Lord Rama will seize your filthy soul and send it flaming into hell – and you'll be born in your next life as the filthy krait you are. Go home and lick up your own blood, you sisterfucker, before I break your neck.' He wrenched the young man's lathi from his grasp and pushed him into the crowd.

His face flaming with anger, Maan now walked with Firoz unharmed through the mob, which seemed a little cowed by his words, a little uncertain of its purpose. Before it could think its way out again, Maan, pushing Firoz in front of him, had walked fifty yards and turned a corner.

'Now run!' he said.

He and Firoz ran for their lives. The mob was still dangerous. It was in effect leaderless for a few minutes and uncertain what to do, but it soon regrouped and, feeling cheated of its prey, moved along the alleys to hunt for more.

Maan knew that at all costs they had to avoid the route of the Bharat Milaap procession and still somehow get to his sister's house. Who knew what danger they might have to face on the way, what other mobs or luna-
tics they might encounter.

'I'll try to get back to the Imambara,' said Firoz.

'It's too late now,' said Maan. 'You're cut off, and you don't know this area. Stay with me now. We're going to my sister's. Her husband's on the Ramlila Committee, no one will attack their house.'

'But I can't. How can I –'

'Shut up!' said Maan, his voice trembling again. 'You've put us through enough danger already. Don't have any more stupid scruples. There's no purdah in our family, thank God. Go through that gate there and don't make a sound.' Then he put his arm around Firoz's shoulder.

He led Firoz through a small washermen's colony, and they emerged in the tiny alley where Kedarnath lived. It was a mere fifty yards from where the stage had been set up for the Bharat Milaap. They could hear the sound of shouting and screaming from close by. Veena's house was in an almost entirely Hindu neighbourhood; no Muslim mobs could range here.

They stared at Firoz as he stumbled into the room in his bloodstained white sherwani – and at Maan, clutching the bloodstained lathi in his hand. Kedarnath stepped forward, the other three shrank back. Old Mrs Tandon clapped her hands to her mouth. 'Hai Ram! Hai Ram!' she gasped in horror.

'Firoz is staying here until we can get him out safely,' said Maan, looking at each of them in turn. 'There's a mob roaming around – and there'll be others. But everyone here is safe. No one will think of attacking this house.'

'But the blood – are you wounded?' asked Veena, turning to Firoz, her eyes distracted with concern.

Maan looked at Firoz's sherwani and his own lathi, and suddenly burst out laughing. 'Yes, this lathi did it, but I didn't – and it's not his blood.'

Firoz greeted his hosts as courteously as his own shock and theirs would allow.

Bhaskar, still tear-faced, seeing the effect of all this on his parents, looked strangely at Maan, who placed the long bamboo staff against the wall, and kissed his nephew on the forehead.

'This is the Nawab Sahib of Baitar's younger son,' said Maan to old Mrs Tandon. She nodded silently. Her mind had turned to the days of Partition in Lahore and her memories and thoughts were those of absolute terror.

4

Firoz changed hurriedly out of his long coat into one of Kedarnath's kurta-pyjamas. Veena made them a quick cup of tea with plenty of sugar. After a while, Maan and Firoz climbed up to the roof, to the pots and plants of the small garden. Maan crushed a small tulsi leaf and put it in his mouth.

As they looked around them they saw that fires had

already broken out here and there in the city. They could make out several of the main buildings of Brahmpur: the spire of the Imambara still ablaze with light – the lights of the Barsaat Mahal, the dome of the Legislative Assembly, the railway station, and – far beyond the Subzipore Club, the fainter glow of the university. But here and there in the old city it was not lights but fire that lit the sky. The muted din of drums came to them from the direction of the Imambara. And distant shouts, more distinct at times as the breeze changed, reached their ears, together with other sounds that could have been firecrackers, but were more likely the sounds of police firing.

'You saved my life,' said Firoz.

Maan embraced him. He smelt of sweat and fear.

'You should have had a wash before you changed,' he said. 'All that running in your sherwani – thank God you're safe.'

'Maan, I must get back. They'll be worried crazy about me at the house. They'll risk their own lives to look for me. . . .'

Suddenly the lights went out at the Imambara.

Firoz said in quiet dread: 'What could have happened there?'

Maan said: 'Nothing.' He was wondering how Saeeda Bai would have got back to Pasand Bagh. Surely she must have remained in the safe area near the Imambara.

The night was warm, but there was a slight breeze. Neither of them said anything for a while.

A large glow now lit the sky about half a mile to the west. This was the lumberyard of a well-known Hindu trader who lived in a predominantly Muslim neighbourhood. Other fires sprang up around it. The drums were silent now, and the sounds of intermittent firing were very clear. Maan was too exhausted to feel any fear. A numbness and a terrible feeling of isolation and helplessness came over him.

Firoz closed his eyes, as if to shut out the terrible vision of the city in flames. But other fires beset his mind – the fire-acrobats of the Moharram fair; the embers of the trench dug outside the Imambara at Baitar House burning with logs and brushwood for ten days, the candelabra of the Imambara at the Fort blazing and guttering as Ustad Majeed Khan sang Raag Darbari while his father nodded with pleasure.

He suddenly got up, agitated.

Someone shouted from a neighbouring rooftop that curfew had been declared.

'How could it be declared?' asked Maan. 'People couldn't have got home by now.' He added softly, 'Firoz, sit down.'

'I don't know,' shouted the man. 'But it has just been announced on the radio that curfew has been declared and that in an hour police will have orders to shoot on sight. Before then, only if they see actual violence.'

'Yes, that makes sense,' Maan shouted back, wondering what if anything made sense any more.

'Who are you? Who's that with you? Kedarnath? Is everyone safe in your family?'

'It's not Kedarnath – it's a friend who came to see the Bharat Milaap. I'm Veena's brother.'

'Well, you'd better not move tonight, if you don't want to get your throat slit by the Muslims – or get shot by the police. What a night. Tonight of all nights.'

'Maan,' said Firoz quietly and urgently, 'can I use your sister's phone?'

'She doesn't have one,' said Maan.

Firoz looked at him with dismay.

'A neighbour's then. I have to get word back to Baitar House. If the news of the curfew is on the radio, my father will hear of it at the Fort in Baitar, and he will be terrified about what's happened here. Imtiaz might try to come back and get a curfew pass. For all I know Murtaza Ali might already be sending out search parties for me, and at a time like this that's crazy. Do you think you might phone from the house of one of Veena's friends?'

'We don't want anyone to know you're here,' said Maan. 'But don't worry, I'll find a way,' he said when he saw the look of sickening anxiety on his friend's face. 'I'll talk to Veena.'

Veena too had memories of Lahore; but her most recent memories were those of losing Bhaskar at the Pul Mela, and she could conceive the Nawab Sahib's agony of mind when he heard that Firoz had not returned home.

'How about trying Priya Agarwal?' said Maan. 'I could go over to her place.'

'Maan, you're not going anywhere,' said his sister. 'Are you mad? It's a five minute walk through the alleys – this isn't why I tied the rakhi around your wrist.' After a minute's thought she said: 'I'll go to the neighbour whose phone I use in an emergency. It's only two rooftops away. You met her that day – she's a good woman, the only trouble is that she is rabidly antiMuslim. Let me think. What's the number of Baitar House?'

Maan told her.

Veena came up to the roof with him, crossed over the connected rooftops, and descended the stairs to her neighbour's house.

Veena's large and voluble neighbour, out of her usual friendliness and curiosity, hung around while Veena made the call. The phone, after all, was in her room. Veena told her she was trying to get in touch with her father.

'But I just saw him at the Bharat Milaap, near the temple –'

'He had to go home. The noise was too much for him. And the smoke was not good for my mother either. Or for Pran's lungs – he didn't come. But Maan is here – he's had a lucky escape from a Muslim mob.'

'It must be providence,' said the woman. 'If they had got hold of him –'

The telephone was not a dialling machine; and Veena had to give the Baitar House number to the operator.

'Oh, you're not calling Prem Nivas?' said the woman, who knew that number from Veena's previous calls.

'No. Baoji had to visit friends later this evening.'

When a voice came on the line Veena said: 'I would like to speak to the Sahib.'

An aged voice at the other end said, 'Which Sahib? The Nawab Sahib or the Burré Sahib or the Chhoté Sahib?'

'Anyone,' said Veena.

'But the Nawab Sahib is in Baitar with the Burré Sahib, and Chhoté Sahib has not yet come home from the Imambara.'

The aged voice – it was Ghulam Rusool – was halting and agitated. 'They say there has been trouble in town, that you can see fires even from the roof of this house. I must go now. There are arrangements –'

'Please be patient –' said Veena quickly. 'I will speak to anyone – put Sahib's secretary on the line – or anyone responsible. Call someone – anyone – to the line, please. This is Mahesh Kapoor's daughter Veena speaking, and I need to pass on an urgent message.'

There was silence for a few seconds, then the young voice of Murtaza Ali came on the line. He sounded both embarrassed and extremely anxious. He had sensed that perhaps there might be some news of Firoz.

Veena said, choosing her words with extreme care: 'I   23

am Mahesh Kapoor's daughter. This is about Sahib's younger son.'

'The Nawab Sahib's younger son? The Chhoté Sahib?'

'Exactly. There is nothing to worry about. He is unharmed, and quite safe, and staying in Misri Mandi tonight. Please inform Sahib of that in case he should inquire.'

'God is merciful!' came the quiet response.

'He will go home tomorrow when curfew is relaxed. Meanwhile, no search parties should be sent out for him. No one should go to the police station to get a curfew pass – or come here – or talk to anyone about his being here. Just say he is staying with me – with his sister.'

'Thank you, Madam, thank you for calling us – we were just about to set out in an armed party – it would have been terrible – we imagined the worst –'

'I must go now,' said Veena, knowing that the longer she talked the more difficult it would be to maintain a protective ambiguity.

'Yes, yes,' said Murtaza Ali. 'Khuda haafiz.'

'Khuda haafiz,' replied Veena without thinking, and put down the phone.

Her neighbour looked at her strangely.

Unwilling to make further conversation with the curious woman, Veena explained that she had to go back home immediately because Bhaskar had sprained his ankle running about; and Maan and her husband needed to be fed; and old Mrs Tandon, with her memories of Pakistan, was in a panic and would need to be soothed.

5

But when she got back to the house, she found her mother-in-law, who was downstairs, almost incoherent with shock. Kedarnath had just gone out into the night, planning, no doubt, to calm down any people he found: to prevent them from harming others and, in case they had not heard about the curfew, themselves.

Veena almost fainted. She leaned against the wall and stared ahead of her. Finally her mother-in-law stopped sobbing and her words began to make more sense.

'He said that in this area there would be no risk from Muslims,' she whispered. 'He wouldn't listen to me. He said that it wasn't Lahore – that he would be back very shortly,' she continued, looking at Veena's face for comfort. '"Very shortly," he said. He said he would be back very shortly.' She broke down once again at the words.

Veena's mouth began to tremble. It was the phrase Kedarnath was fond of using when he went away on his interminable sales trips.

There was no comfort for the old lady to be found in Veena's face. 'Why didn't you stop him? Why didn't Maan stop him?' she cried. She was furious at her husband for this selfish and irresponsible heroism. Did she and Bhaskar and his mother not exist for him?

'Maan was on the roof,' said the old lady.

Now Bhaskar came down the stairs. Something had obviously been troubling him for a while.

'Why did Firoz Maama have so much blood all over him?' he demanded. 'Did Maan Maama beat him up? He said he didn't. But he was holding the lathi.'

'Be quiet, Bhaskar,' said Veena in a desperate voice. 'Go upstairs at once. Go upstairs and back to bed. Everything's all right. I'm here if you need me.' She gave him a hug.

Bhaskar wanted to know exactly what the matter was. 'Nothing,' said Veena. 'I have to prepare some food – don't get in my way.' She knew that if Maan got to know about what had happened he would immediately go out to look for his brother-in-law and would put himself at very grievous risk. Kedarnath at least did know exactly where the Hindu areas ended. But she was tormented with anxiety for him. Before Bhaskar had come down she had been on the verge of going out herself. Now she just waited – the most difficult thing of all.

She quickly heated some food for Maan and Firoz, and took it up, pausing on the stairs in order to appear calm.

Maan smiled when he saw her.

'It's quite warm,' said Maan. 'We'll sleep together on the roof. Just give us a mattress and a light quilt, and we'll be fine. Firoz will need a wash, and I could do with one too. Is something wrong?'

Veena shook her head. 'He almost gets killed, then asks me if something is wrong.'

She took a light quilt out of a trunk, and shook out from its folds the dried neem leaves that she used to preserve winter clothing from pests.

'Sometimes the night flowers on the roof attract insects,' she warned them.

'We'll be fine,' said Firoz. 'I am so grateful to you.'

Veena shook her head. 'Sleep well,' she said.

Kedarnath returned home five minutes before curfew. Veena wept, and refused to speak to him. She buried her face in his scarred hands.

For an hour or so Maan and Firoz remained awake. It felt as if the world was trembling beneath them. The distant sound of gunfire had died down, probably as a result of the imposition of curfew, but the glow from the fires, especially to the west, continued through the night.

6

On Sharad Purnima, the brightest night of the year, Pran and Savita hired a boat and went up the Ganga to look at the Barsaat Mahal. Curfew had been lifted that morning. Mrs Rupa Mehra had advised them not to go, but Savita said that no one could set fire to the river.

'And it isn't good for Pran's asthma either,' added Mrs Rupa Mehra, who believed that he should be confined to his bed and his rocking-chair, and not over-exert himself.

Pran had in fact slowly recovered from the worst of his illness. He was still not able to play cricket, but had built up his strength by walking, at first only around the garden, then a few hundred yards, and finally around campus or along the Ganga. He had avoided the incendiary festivities of Dussehra, and would have to avoid the firecrackers of Divali. But his trouble had not recurred in its acute form, and he had for the most part not allowed it to interfere with his academic work. Some days, when he was feeling weaker, he sat and lectured. His students were protective of him, and even his overworked colleagues on the disciplinary committee tried to relieve him of whatever duties they could.

Tonight, in particular, he felt much better. He reflected on Maan and Firoz's providential escape – and indeed Kedarnath's as well – and was inclined to minimize his own problems.

'Don't worry, Ma,' he reassured his mother-in-law. 'If anything, the river air will do me good. It's still quite warm.'

'Well, it won't be warm on the river. You should take a shawl each. Or a blanket,' grumbled Mrs Rupa Mehra.

After a pause, she said to Lata: 'Why are you looking like that? Do you have a headache?'

28   'No, Ma, I don't, please let me read.'

She had been thinking: thank God Maan is safe.

'What are you reading?' persisted her mother.

'Ma!'

'Bye, Lata, bye, Ma,' said Pran. 'Keep your knitting needles out of Uma's clutches.'

Mrs Rupa Mehra made a sound that was almost a grunt. She believed that one shouldn't mention such unspeakable dangers. She was knitting booties for the baby in the expectation of colder weather.

Pran and Savita walked down to the river, Pran leading the way with a torch, and helping Savita with a hand where the path was steep. He warned her to watch out for the roots of the banyan tree.

The boatman they hired from near the dhobi-ghat happened to be the same one who had taken Lata and Kabir to see the Barsaat Mahal some months previously at dawn. As usual he demanded an outrageous price. Pran brought it down slightly, but was in no mood for further haggling. He was glad Uma was too small to come with them; he was happy to be alone with Savita if only for an hour or two.

The river was still high, and a pleasant breeze was blowing.

'Ma was right – it is cold – you'd better hold onto me for warmth,' Pran said.

'Aren't you going to recite a ghazal by Mast for me?' asked Savita as she looked out, past the ghats and the Fort towards the vague silhouette of the Barsaat Mahal.

'Sorry, you've married the wrong brother,' said Pran.

'No, I don't think so,' said Savita. She leaned her head against his shoulder. 'What is that thing there with the walls and chimney – beyond the Barsaat Mahal?'

'Hmm – I don't know – perhaps the tannery or the shoe factory,' said Pran. 'But everything looks different from this side, especially at night.'

They were silent for a while.

'What's the latest on that front?' said Pran.

'You mean Haresh?'

'Yes.'

'I don't know. Lata's being secretive. But he does write and she does reply. You're the one who's met him. You said you liked him.'

'Well, it's impossible to judge someone on the basis of a single meeting,' said Pran.

'Oh, so you think so!' said Savita archly, and they both laughed.

A thought struck Pran.

'I suppose I too am going to be judged soon enough on the basis of a single meeting,' he said.

'Soon enough!' said Savita.

'Well, things really are going ahead at last –'

'Or so Professor Mishra assures you.'

'No, no – in a month or two at the latest they're going to have their interviews – someone who works in the Registrar's Office mentioned it to one of my father's ex-PAs. So let's see, it's the middle of October now –' Pran looked across towards the burning ghat. He lost the thread of his thoughts.

'How quiet the city looks,' he said. 'And when you think that Maan and Firoz could have been murdered –'

'Don't.'

'Sorry, darling. Anyway, what were you saying?'

'I've forgotten.'

'Oh, well.'

'I think,' said Savita, 'that you're in danger of becoming complacent.'

'Who – me?' said Pran, surprised rather than affronted. 'Why should I be complacent? A humble university lecturer with a weak heart, who will have to puff his way up the cliff at the end of this boat-ride.'

'Well, perhaps not,' said Savita. 'Anyway, what does it feel like to have a wife and child?'

'What does it feel like? It feels wonderful.'

Savita smiled into the darkness. She had fished for a compliment, and landed one.

'This is where you'll get the best view,' said the boatman, driving his long pole deep into the bed of the river. 'I can't go further back into the current. The river's too high.'

'And I suppose it must be quite pleasant to have a husband and child,' added Pran.

'Yes,' said Savita thoughtfully. 'It is.' After a while she said: 'Sad about Meenakshi.'

'Yes. But you've never been very fond of her, have you?'

Savita did not reply.

'Has her miscarriage made you like her more?' said Pran.

'What a question! It has, in a way. Well, let me think about that. I'll know immediately when I see her again.'

'You know,' said Pran, 'I don't look forward to staying with your brother and sister-in-law over the New Year.' He closed his eyes; there was a mild and pleasant breeze on the river.

'I'm not sure there'll even be room for all of us at Sunny Park,' said Savita. 'Ma and Lata can stay with them as usual. And you and I can camp in the garden. Rock-a-bye Baby can hang from the tree-top.'

Pran laughed. 'Well, at least the baby doesn't take after your brother, as I feared she might.'

'Which one?'

'Either. But I meant Arun. Well, they'll have to put us up somewhere – I suppose at the Chatterjis'. I liked that boy, what's his name –'

'Amit?'

'No, the other one – the holy man who was fond of Scotch.'

'Dipankar.'

'Yes, that's it. . . . At any rate, you'll meet him when we go to Calcutta in December,' said Pran.

'But I've already met him,' Savita pointed out. 'At the Pul Mela, most recently.'

'I meant Haresh. You can appraise him at your leisure.'

'But you were just talking about Dipankar.'

'Was I, dear?'

'Really, Pran, I wish you would keep track of your conversation. It's very confusing. I'm sure this isn't how you lecture.'

'I lecture rather well,' said Pran, 'even if I say so myself. But don't take my word for it. Ask Malati.'

'I have no intention of asking Malati how you lecture. The last time she listened to you, you were so overcome you fainted away.'

The boatman was getting tired of holding his boat steady against the current. 'Do you want to talk or to watch the Barsaat Mahal?' he asked. 'You're paying me good money to come here.'

'Yes, yes, of course,' said Pran vaguely.

'You should have come here three nights ago,' said the boatman – 'there were fires burning all along there. Beautiful it looked, and you couldn't smell it here on the Ganga. And the next day lots of corpses at the ghat there. Too many for one ghat to handle. The municipality has been planning another burning ghat for years now but they'll never get down to deciding where.'

'Why?' Pran couldn't resist asking.

'If it's on the Brahmpur side it'll face north like this one. Of course, by rights it should face south, in the direction of Yama. But that would put it on the other shore, and they'd have to ferry the bodies – and the passengers – across.'

'They. You mean you.'

'I suppose so. I wouldn't complain.'

For a while Pran and Savita looked at the Barsaat Mahal, lit in the full light of the full moon. Beautiful by itself, its reflection at night made it look lovelier than ever. The moon shivered gently in the water. The boatman said nothing further.

Another boat passed them. For some reason Pran shuddered.

'What's the matter, darling?'

'Nothing.'

Savita took a small coin out of her purse and put it in Pran's hand.

'Well, what I was thinking was how peaceful it all looks.'

Savita nodded to herself in the darkness. Pran suddenly realized she was crying.

'What's the matter, darling? What have I said?'

'Nothing. I'm so happy. I'm just happy.'

'How strange you are,' said Pran, stroking her hair.

The boatman released his pole and, guided only casually by him, the boat began to move downstream again. Quietly they moved down the calm and sacred river that had come down to earth so that its waters might flow over the ashes of those long dead, and that would continue to flow long after the human race had, through hatred and knowledge, burned itself out.

7

For the last few weeks Mahesh Kapoor had been in two minds – two uncertain and troubled minds – about whether to go back to the Congress Party. He, who was so full of definite, often dismissive, opinion, had found himself lost in a dust-storm of indecision.

Too many factors were whirling around in his head and each time they came to rest they formed a new configuration.

What the Chief Minister had said to him in his garden; what the Nawab Sahib had said to him at the Fort; the visit to Prem Nivas of the seceder from U.P. who had rejoined the Congress; Baba's advice in Debaria; Nehru's coup; Rafi Sahib's circuitous return to the fold; his own beloved legislation which he wanted to make sure did not merely moulder on the statute-books; irritatingly enough, even his wife's unspoken but palpable view of the whole matter: all these told him to go back to the party that, until his slow but thorough disillusionment, had unquestionably been his home.

Things had doubtless changed greatly since that disillusionment. And yet, when he thought about it deeply, how much had really changed? Could he belong in a

party that contained – could he bear to belong to a government that might possibly be run by – the likes of the
present Home Minister? The list of Congress candidates
that was being drawn up in the state did nothing to
dispel his disillusionment. Nor, after his talk with his
old Parliamentary Secretary, could he honestly claim to
himself that he sensed in Nehru any new surge of
decisiveness. Nehru could not even ensure the passage
of his favourite bill through Parliament. Compromise
and muddle had reigned, and compromise and muddle
would reign.

And having once made his break, thought Mahesh
Kapoor, would he not be displaying the very indecisive-
ness he usually condemned by returning? After decades
of loyalty to one party, he who believed in principle and
firmness would have turned his coat twice in the course
of a few months. Kidwai may have returned, but Kripal-
ani had not. Whose had been the more honourable
course?

Angry at himself for his own uncharacteristic dither-
ing, Mahesh Kapoor told himself that he had had enough
time and enough advice to determine twenty such matters. Whatever he decided, there would be aspects of his
decision he would find difficult to live with. He should
stop fretting, examine the nub of the matter, and once
and for all say Yes or No.

Yet what, if anything, was the nub?

Was it the zamindari legislation? Was it his dread

of communal hatred and violence? Was it the real and delicious possibility that he, not Agarwal, might become Chief Minister? Was it the fear that if he remained outside the Congress, he would lose his seat – that he could maintain his purity only in the wilderness? Surely all these things pointed in the same direction. What was really holding him back but uncertainty and pride?

He stared unseeingly out from his small office towards the garden of Prem Nivas.

His wife had his tea sent to him; it went cold.

She came to ask him if he was all right and brought another cup for him herself. She said: 'So you have decided to return to the Congress? That's good.'

He responded with exasperation: 'I have decided nothing. What makes you think I have?'

'After Maan and Firoz nearly –'

'Maan and Firoz have nothing to do with it. I have been thinking this matter over for weeks without coming to any conclusion.' He looked at her in amazement.

She stirred his tea once more and placed it on the table, which was easier to do these days, since it was not covered with files.

Mahesh Kapoor sipped it and said nothing.

After a while he said, 'Leave me alone. I am not going to discuss this matter with you. Your presence is distracting me. I don't know where your farfetched intuitions 37 come from. But they are more inaccurate and suspect than astrology.'

8

Less than a week after the riots in Brahmpur, the Prime Minister of Pakistan, Liaquat Ali Khan, was shot at a public meeting that he was addressing at Rawalpindi. The murderer was done to death on the spot by the crowd.

At the news of his death, all government flags were lowered to half-mast in Brahmpur. The university court convened a meeting to express its condolences. In a city where the memory of rioting was only a week old, this had something of a sobering effect.

The Nawab Sahib was back in Brahmpur when he heard the news. He had known Liaquat Ali well, since both Baitar House and Baitar Fort had been meeting places for Muslim League leaders in his father's time. He looked at some of the old photographs of those conferences and read through some of the old correspondence between his father and Liaquat Ali. He realized – though he did not see what he could do about the fact – that he had begun to live increasingly in the past.

For the Nawab Sahib Partition had been a multiple tragedy: many of those he knew, both Muslim and Hindu, had been killed or injured or scarred by the terror of those days; he had lost two parts of his country; his family had been broken up by migration; Baitar House had come under attack through manipulations of the evacuee property laws; most of the great estate surrounding Baitar Fort was soon to be wrested from him under zamindari laws that would have been almost impossible to pass in a united India; the language of his ancestors and favourite poets was under siege; and he was conscious that even his patriotism was no longer readily accepted by many of his acquaintances. He thanked God that he still had friends like Mahesh Kapoor who understood him; and he thanked God that his son had friends like Mahesh Kapoor's son. But he felt beleaguered and beset by what was happening around him; and he reflected that if this was what he felt, it must be infinitely worse for those of his religion less insulated from the hardships of the world than himself.

I suppose I am getting old, he said to himself, and querulousness is a standard symptom of senility. He could not help grieving, though, for the cultivated, level-headed Liaquat Ali, whom he had personally liked. Nor, though he had hated the thought of Pakistan once, could he turn away from it with unconcern now that it actually existed. When the Nawab Sahib thought about Pakistan, it was about West Pakistan. Many of his old friends were there, many of his relatives, many of the places of which he had warm recollections. That Jinnah should have died in the first year of Pakistan's life, and Liaquat Ali early in its fifth was no happy augury for a country that needed, more than anything else, experience in its leadership and moderation in its polity, and appeared now to be bereft of both.

The Nawab Sahib, saddened by things and feeling a stranger in the world, phoned Mahesh Kapoor to invite him over for lunch the next day.

'Please persuade Mrs Mahesh Kapoor to come as well. I will get her food from outside, of course.'

'I can't. The mad woman will be fasting for my health tomorrow. It's Karva Chauth, and she can't eat from sunrise till moonrise. Or drink a drop of water. If she does I'll die.'

'That would be unfortunate, Kapoor Sahib. There has been too much killing and dying of late,' said the Nawab Sahib. 'How is Maan, by the way?' he inquired fondly.

'Much the same. But recently I've stopped telling him three times a day to return to Banaras. There's something to be said for the boy.'

'There's a great deal to be said for the boy,' said the Nawab Sahib.

'Oh, it would have been the same the other way around,' said Mahesh Kapoor. 'Anyway, I've been thinking about my son's advice regarding constituencies. And your advice, of course, as well.'

'And about parties too, I hope.'

There was a long silence on the line.

'Yes, well, I've decided to rejoin the Congress. You're the first to know,' said Mahesh Kapoor.

The Nawab Sahib sounded pleased.

'Fight from Baitar, Kapoor Sahib,' he said. 'Fight from Baitar. You'll win, Inshallah – and with the help of your friends.'

'Let's see, let's see.'

'So you'll come for lunch tomorrow?'

'Yes, yes. What's the occasion?'

'No occasion. Just do me the favour of sitting silently through the meal and hearing me complain about how much better things were in the old days.'

'All right.'

'Give my greetings to Maan's mother,' said the Nawab Sahib. He paused. It would have been more proper to say 'Pran's mother' or even 'Veena's mother'. He stroked his beard, then continued: 'But, Kapoor Sahib, is it a sensible idea for her to fast in her present state of health?'

'Sensible!' was Mahesh Kapoor's response. 'Sensible! My dear Nawab Sahib, you are talking a language that is foreign to her.'

9

This language was also presumably foreign to Mrs Rupa Mehra, who stopped knitting the baby's booties on the day of Karva Chauth. Indeed, she locked up her knitting needles together with any sewing and darning needles that were lying about the house. Her reason was simple. Savita was fasting until moonrise for her husband's health and longevity, and touching a needle, even inadvertently, on that day would be disastrous.

One year an unfortunate young woman, famished during her fast, was persuaded by her anxious brothers that the moon had risen when all they had done was to light a fire behind a tree to simulate the moonglow. She had eaten a little before she had realized the trick, and soon enough the news was brought to her of her husband's sudden death. He had been pierced through and through by thousands of needles. By performing many austerities and making many offerings to the goddesses, the young widow had finally extracted their promise that if she kept the fast properly the next year her husband would return to life. Each day for the whole year she removed the needles one by one from her husband's lifeless body. The very last one, however, was removed on the day of Karva Chauth itself by a maid-servant just as her master came back to life. Since she was the first woman he saw after opening his eyes, he believed that it was through her pains that he had revived. He had no choice but to discard his wife and marry her. Needles on Karva Chauth were therefore fearfully inauspicious: touch a needle and lose a husband.

What Savita, fortified in logic by law-books and

grounded in reality by her baby, thought of all this, was not obvious. But she observed Karva Chauth to the letter, even going to the extent of first viewing the rising moon through a sieve.

The Sahib and Memsahib of Calcutta, on the other hand, considered Karva Chauth a signal idiocy, and were unmoved by Mrs Rupa Mehra's frantic implorations that Meenakshi – even if Brahmo by family – should observe it. 'Really, Arun,' said Meenakshi. 'Your mother does go on about things.'

One by one the Hindu festivals fell, some observed fervently, some lukewarmly, some merely noted, some entirely ignored. On five consecutive days around the end of October came Dhanteras, Hanuman Jayanti, Divali, Annakutam, and Bhai Duj. The day immediately following was observed most religiously by Pran, who kept his ear to the radio for hours: it was the first day of the first Test Match of the cricket season, played in Delhi against a visiting English side.

A week later the gods at last awoke from their four months' slumber, having wisely slept through a very boring and slow-scoring draw.

10

But though India vs England was humdrum in the extreme, the same could not be said for the University vs

Old Brahmpurians match held that Sunday at the university cricket ground.

The university team was not quite as good as it might have been, owing to a couple of injuries. Nor were the Old Brahmpurians a push-over, for their side contained not merely the usual players rustled up from here and there, but also two men who had captained the university in the last ten years or so.

Among the rustled, however, was Maan. Among the uninjured was Kabir. And Pran was one of the umpires.

It was a brilliant, clear, crisp, early November day, and the grass was still fresh and green. The mood was festive, and – with exams and other woes a million miles away – the students were out in force. They cheered and booed and stood around the field talking to the outfielders and generally creating as much excitement off the field as on. A few teachers could be seen among them.

One of these was Dr Durrani; he found cricket curiously fertile. At the moment, unmoved by the fact that his son had just bowled Maan out with a leg-break, he was thinking about the hexadic, octal, decimal and duodecimal systems and attempting to work out their various advantages.

He turned to a colleague:

'Interesting, er, wouldn't you say, Patwardhan, that the number six, which, though "perfect", has a, well, an

almost fugitive existence in mathematics – except, er, in

geometry, of course, should um, be the – the presiding, one might say, the presiding, um, deity of cricket, wouldn't you say?'

Sunil Patwardhan nodded but would not say. His eyes were glued to the pitch. The next player was no sooner in than out; he had been dispatched on Kabir's next ball: a googly this time. A huge roar of delight rose from the crowd.

'Six balls to an, um, over, don't you see, Patwardhan, six runs to a boundary, a, a lofted boundary, of course, and, um, six stumps on the, er, field!'

The incoming player had hardly had time to pad up. The previous batsman was already back in the pavilion by the time he walked out onto the field, flexing his bat impatiently and aggressively. He was one of the two former captains, and he was damned if he was going to provide Kabir with a hat-trick. In he went and fiercely he glared, in a sweep that encompassed not only the tense but appraising bowler, but also his own batting partner, the opposite stumps, the umpire, and a few innocuous mynas.

Like Arjun aiming his arrow at the eye of the invisible bird, Kabir stared down single-mindedly at the invisible middle stump of his adversary. Straight down the pitch came the ball, but deceptively slowly this time. The batsman tried to play it. He missed; and the dull thump of the ball as it hit his pad was like the sound of muffled doom.

Eleven voices appealed in triumphant delight, and Pran, smiling, raised his finger in the air.

He nodded at Kabir, who was grinning broadly and accepting the congratulations of his team-mates.

The cheering of the crowd took more than a minute to die down, and continued sporadically for the rest of Kabir's over. Sunil executed a few swift steps of joy – a sort of kathak jig. He looked at Dr Durrani to see what effect his son's triumph had had on him.

Dr Durrani was frowning in concentration, his eyebrows working up and down.

'Curious, though, isn't it, um, Patwardhan, that the number, er, six should be, um, embodied in one of the most, er, er, beautiful, er, shapes in all nature: I refer, um, needless to say, to the er, benzene ring with its single and, er, double carbon bonds. But is it, er, truly symmetrical, Patwardhan, or, um, asymmetrical? Or asymmetrically symmetrical, perhaps, like those, er, sub-super-operations of the, er, Pergolesi Lemma ... not really like the, er, rather unsatisfactory petals of an, um, iris. Curious, wouldn't you say ...?'

'Most curious,' agreed Sunil.

*

Savita was talking to Firoz:

'Of course, it's different for you, Firoz, I don't mean because you're a man as such, but because, well, you don't have a baby to distract you from your clients. Or perhaps that comes to the same thing.... I was talking to Jaya Sood the other day, and she tells me that there are bats – and I don't mean cricket bats! – in the High Court bathroom. When I told her I couldn't bear the thought, she said, ' "Well, if you're frightened of bats, why are you doing law in the first place?" But, do you know, though I never imagined I would, I actually find law interesting now, really interesting. Not like this awful sleepy game. They haven't made a run for the last ten minutes.... Oh no, I've just dropped a stitch, I always feel drowsy in the sun.... I simply can't see what Pran sees in it, or why he insists on ignoring all of us for five days with his ear glued to the radio, or being a referee and standing in the sun the whole day, but do you think my protests have any effect? ' "Standing in the sun is good for me," he insists.... Or Maan, for that matter. Before lunch he runs from one wicket to the other seven times, and now after lunch he runs along the edge of the field for a few minutes at the most, and that's that: the whole Sunday's gone! You're very sensible to stick to polo, Firoz – at least that's over in an hour – and you do get some exercise.'

Firoz was thinking about Maan:

My dearest, dearest Maan, you've saved my life all right and I love you dearly, but if you keep nattering to Lata, your captain will forfeit your own.

Maan was talking to Lata:

'No, no, it's all right to talk, no ball ever comes my way. They know what a fantastic player I am, so they've put me here on the boundary where I can't drop any catches or overthrow the ball or anything. And if I go off to sleep, it doesn't matter. Do you know, I think you're looking very beautiful today, no, don't make a face. I've always thought so – green suits you, you know. You just merge with the grass like a ... a nymph! a peri in paradise.... No, no, not at all, I think we're doing tremendously well. All out for 219 isn't bad, after such a poor beginning, and now we've got them at 157 for 7. They've got hopeless people at the bottom of their batting order. I don't think they have a chance.... The Old Brahmpurians haven't won in a decade, so it'll be a great victory! The only danger is this wretched Durrani fellow, who's still batting on at ... what does the scoreboard say? 68.... Once we've forked him off the pitch we'll be home and dry....'

Lata was thinking about Kabir:

O spirit of love! how quick and fresh art thou,
That notwithstanding thy capacity
Receiveth as the sea, nought enters there,
Of what validity and pitch soe'er
But falls into abatement and low price....

A few mynas were sitting on the field, their faces turned

towards the batsmen, and the mild, warm sun shone down on her as the sound of bat on ball continued drowsily – interspersed occasionally by a cheer – through the late afternoon. She broke off a blade of grass, and moved it gently up and down her arm.

Kabir was talking to Pran:
   'Thanks; no, the light's fine, Dr Kapoor ... oh, thank you – well, it was just a fluke this morning....'

Pran was thinking about Savita:
   I know our whole Sunday's gone, darling, but next Sunday I'll do whatever you want. I promise. If you wish, I'll hold a huge ball of wool instead, while you knit twenty booties for the baby.

*

Kabir had gone in fourth, higher up than usual in the batting order, but had more than justified himself there. He had noticed Lata in the crowd, but this had the effect, oddly enough, of steadying his nerves – or increasing his determination. His score mounted, mainly through boundaries, not a few of which got past Maan, and it now stood in the nineties.

One by one his partners had dropped away, however, and the fall of wickets told its own story: 140 for 4, 143 for 5, 154 for 6, 154 for 7, 183 for 8, and now 190 for 9. There were 29 runs to score for a tie, 30 for a win, and his new partner was the exceedingly nervous wicket-keeper! Too bad, thought Kabir. He's lived so long behind the stumps that he doesn't know what to do with himself when he's in front of them. Luckily it's the beginning of the over. Still, he'll be out the first ball he faces, poor chap. The whole thing's impossible, but I wonder if I'll at least manage to get my century.

The wicket-keeper, however, played an admirable second fiddle, and Kabir got the strategic singles that enabled him to keep the bowling. When the University stood at 199, with his own score at 98, on the last ball of the last-but-one over – with three minutes to go before end of play – he tried to make his usual single. As he and his partner passed each other, he said: 'We'll draw it yet!'

A cheer had gone up for the anticipated 200 while they were still running. The fielder hurled the ball at Kabir's wicket. It missed by a hair, but hurtled onwards with such force that poor Maan, who had begun, gallantly, to clap, realized too late what was happening. Too late did he run towards it, too late did he try to hurl himself at it as it sped past his extended length to the boundary.

A great cheer rose from the university ranks – but whether for Kabir's fortuitous five off a single ball, or for his century, or for the university's double-century, or for the fact that with sixteen, rather than twenty, runs to win in the last over, they suddenly felt they still had a chance, no one could say.

The captain of the Old Brahmpurians, a major from the cantonment, glared at Maan.

But now, to a background of cheers and jeers and shouts, Kabir faced the final over. He hit a grand cover drive for four, lofted the next ball just over long on for another, and faced the third ball to a complete and petrified silence from spectators of both sides alike.

It was a good-length ball. He hit it towards mid-wicket, but the moment he realized it was only worth a single, he waved his partner urgently back.

They ran two on the next ball.

It was now the last ball but one, with five runs to tie and six to win. No one dared to breathe. No one had the least idea of what Kabir was aiming to do – or the bowler for that matter. Kabir passed his gloved hand through his wavy hair. Pran thought he looked unnaturally calm at the crease.

Perhaps the bowler had succumbed to his tension and frustration, for amazingly enough his next ball was a full-toss. Kabir, with a smile on his face and happiness in his heart, hit it high in the air with all the force he could muster, and watched it as it sailed in a serene parabola towards victory.

High, high, high it rose in the air, carrying with it all the joy and hopes and blessings of the university. A murmur, not yet a cheer, arose all around, and then swelled into a shout of triumph.

But, as Kabir watched, a dreadful thing happened. For

Maan, who too had been watching the red grenade ascend and then descend, and whose mouth was open in an expression of trance-like dismay, suddenly found himself at the very edge of the boundary, almost leaning backwards. And, to his considerable amazement, the ball lay in his hands.

The cheer became a sudden silence, then a great collective groan, to be replaced by an amazed shout of victory by the Old Brahmpurians. A finger moved skywards. The bails were taken off. The players stood dazed in the field, shaking hands and shaking heads. And Maan somersaulted five times for sheer joy in the direction of the spectators.

*

What a goof! thought Lata, watching Maan. Perhaps I should elope with him next April 1st.

'How's that? How's that? How's that?' Maan asked Firoz, hugging him, then rushed back to his team to be applauded as the hero of the day.

Firoz noticed Savita raise her eyebrows. He raised his eyebrows back at her; he wondered what she had made of the soporific climax.

'Still awake – just about,' Savita said, smiling at Pran as he came off the field a few minutes later.

A nice fellow – plucky under pressure, thought Pran, watching Kabir detach himself from his friends and walk 52 towards them, his bat under his arm. A pity....

'Fluke of a catch,' murmured Kabir disgustedly, almost under his breath, as he passed Lata on his way back to the pavilion.

11

The Hindu festive season was almost over. But for Brahmpur one festival, observed much more devotedly here than almost anywhere in India, that of Kartik Purnima, remained. The full moon of Kartik brings to an end one of the three especially sacred months for bathing; and since Brahmpur lies on the holiest river of all, many pious people observe their daily dip throughout the month, eat their single meal, worship the tulsi plant, and hang lamps suspended from the end of bamboo poles in small baskets to guide departed souls across the sky. As the Puranas say: 'What fruit was obtained in the Perfect Age by doing austerities for one hundred years, all that is obtained by a bath in the Five Rivers during the month of Kartik.'

It is of course also possible that the city of Brahmpur could be said to have a special claim on this festival because of the god whose name the city bears. A seventeenth century commentator on the Mahabharata wrote: 'Brahma's festival is celebrated by all, and is held in autumn when the corn has begun to grow.' Certainly in Pushkar, the greatest living shrine to Brahma in all India

53

(indeed, the only one of any great significance other than Gaya and – possibly – Brahmpur), it is Kartik Purnima that is the time of the great camel fair and the visit of tens of thousands of pilgrims. The image of Brahma in the great temple there is daubed with orange paint and decorated with tinsel by his devotees in the manner of other gods. Perhaps the strong observance of the festival in Brahmpur is a residue of the time when Brahma was worshipped here too, in his own city, as a bhakti god, a god of personal devotion, before he was displaced in this role by Shiva – or by Vishnu in one or other of his incarnations.

A residue is all it is, however, because for most of the year one would not suspect Brahma to be a presence in Brahmpur at all. It is his rivals – or colleagues – of the trinity who hold the limelight. The Pul Mela or the Chandrachur Temple speak of the power of Shiva, whether as the source of the Ganga or as the great sensual ascetic symbolized by the linga. As for Vishnu: the notable presence of numerous Krishna devotees (such as Sanaki Baba) and the fervent celebration (by those like Mrs Mahesh Kapoor) of Janamashtami bear witness to his presence as Krishna; and his presence as Rama is unmistakable not only during Ramnavami early in the year but during the nine nights culminating in Dussehra, when Brahmpur is part of an island of Rama worship in a sea of goddess worship that extends from Bengal to Gujarat.

Why Brahma, the Self-Created or Egg-born, the overseer of sacrifice, the Supreme Creator, the old four-faced god who set in motion the triple world, should have suffered eclipse over the centuries is unclear. At one time even Shiva is shown cringing in the Mahabharata before him; and it is from a common root with Brahma himself that the words not only for 'brahmin' but also for 'brahman', the world-soul, derive. But by the time of the late Puranas, not to mention modern times, his influence had waned to a shadow.

Perhaps it was because – unlike Shiva or Rama or Krishna or Durga or Kali – he was never associated with youth or beauty or terror, those well-springs of personal devotion. Perhaps it was because he was too far above suffering and yearning to satisfy the longing of the heart for an identifiably human ideal or intercessor – one perhaps who had come down to earth to suffer with the rest of mankind in order that righteousness might be established. Perhaps it was because certain myths surrounding him – for instance his creation of mankind by intercourse with his own daughter – were too difficult to accept by a constant following over long ages and changing mores.

Or perhaps it was that, refusing to be turned on and off like a tap by requests for intercession, Brahma at last refused to deliver what was asked of him by millions of upraised hands, and therefore fell out of favour. It is rare for religious feeling to be entirely transcendent, and Hindus as much as anyone else, perhaps more so, are eager for terrestrial, not merely post-terrestrial, blessings.

We want specific results, whether to cure a child of disease or to guarantee his IAS results, whether to ensure the birth of a son or to find a suitable match for a daughter. We go to a temple to be blessed by our chosen deity before a journey, and have our account books sanctified by Kali or Saraswati. At Divali, the words 'shubh laabh' – auspicious profit – are seen on the walls of every newly whitewashed shop; while Lakshmi, the presiding goddess, smiles from a poster as she sits on her lotus, serene and beautiful, dispensing gold coins from one of her four arms.

It must be admitted that there are those, mainly Shaivites and Vaishnavites, who claim that Brahmpur has nothing to do with the god Brahma at all – that the name is a corruption of Bahrampur or Brahminpur or Berhampur or some other such name, whether Islamic or Hindu. But for one reason or another these theories may be discarded. The evidence of coins, of inscriptions, of historical records and travellers' accounts from Hsuen Tsang to Al-Biruni, from Babur to Tavernier, not to mention those of British travellers, provide ample evidence of the ancient name of the city.

It should be mentioned in passing that the spelling Brahmpore, which the British insisted on imposing on the city, was converted back to its more phonetic transcription when the name of the state itself was changed to Purva Pradesh under the Protected Provinces (Alteration of Name) Order, 1949, which came into operation a few months before the commencement of the Constitution. The spelling Brumpore was the source, however, of not a few errors by amateur etymologists during the two centuries of its prevalence.

There are even a few misguided souls who assert that the name Brahmpur is a variant of Bhrampur – the city of illusion or error. But the proper response to this hypothesis is that there are always people willing to believe anything, however implausible, merely in order to be contrary.

12

'Pran darling, please turn off that light.'

The switch was near the door.

Pran yawned. 'Oh, I'm too sleepy,' was his response.

'But I can't sleep with it on,' said Savita.

'What if I had been sitting in the other room, working late? Wouldn't you have been able to do it yourself?'

'Yes, of course, darling,' yawned Savita, 'but you're closer to the door.'

Pran got out of bed, switched off the light, and staggered back.

'The moment Pran darling appears,' he said, 'a use is found for him.'

'Pran, you're so lovable,' said Savita.

'Of course! Anyone would be who dances attendance. But when Malati Trivedi finds me lovable....'

'As long as you don't find her lovable....'

And they drifted off to sleep.

At two in the morning the phone rang.

The insistent double ring pierced their dreams. Pran woke up with a shock. The baby woke up and started crying. Savita hushed her.

'Good heavens! Who could that be?' cried Savita, startled. 'It'll wake up the whole house – at – what's the time? – I hope it's nothing serious –'

Pran had stumbled out of the room.

'Hello?' he said, picking up the receiver. 'Hello, Pran Kapoor here.'

There was the sound of thick breathing at the other end. Then a voice rasped out:

'Good! This is Marh.'

'Yes?' said Pran, trying to keep his voice low. Savita had got out of bed. He shook his head to reassure her that it was nothing serious and when she left he closed the dining room door.

'This is Marh! The Raja of Marh.'

'Yes, yes, I understand. Yes, Your Highness, what can I do for you?'

'You know exactly what you can do for me.'

'I am sorry, Your Highness, but if this is about your son's expulsion, there's nothing I can tell you. You've received a letter from the university –'

'You – you – do you know who I am?'

'Perfectly, Your Highness. Now it is somewhat late –'

'You listen to me, if you don't want something to happen to you – or to someone who matters to you. You rescind that order.'

'Your Highness, I –'

'Just because of some prank – and I know that your brother is just as – my son tells me he turned him upside down and shook the money out of his pockets when he was gambling – you tell your brother – and your land-robbing father –'

'My father?'

'Your whole family needs to be taught a lesson –'

The baby started to cry again. A note of fury appeared in the voice of the Raja of Marh.

'Is that your baby?'

Pran was silent.

'Did you hear me?'

'Your Highness, I would like to forget this conversation. But if you phone me up again at this hour without cause, or if I receive any further threats from you, I will have to report the matter to the police.'

'Without cause? – you expel my son for a prank –'

'Your Highness, this was not some prank. The university authorities made the facts quite clear in their letter to you. Taking part in a communal riot is not a prank. Your son is lucky that he is still alive and out of jail.'

'He must graduate. He must. He has bathed in the Ganga – he is now a snaatak.'

'That was somewhat premature,' Pran said, trying to keep the scorn out of his voice. 'And your distress on that count cannot be expected to outweigh the decision of the committee. Goodnight, Your Highness.'

'Not so quick! You listen to me now – I know you voted to expel him.'

'That is neither here nor there, Your Highness – I saved him from trouble once before, but –'

'It is very much here and there. When my temple is completed – do you know that it will be my son, my son whom you are trying to martyr, who will lead the ceremonies – and that the wrath of Shiva –'

Pran put down the phone. He sat down at the dining table for a minute or two, staring at it and shaking his head.

'Who was that?' asked Savita when he returned to bed.

'Oh, no one, some lunatic who wanted to get his son admitted to the university,' said Pran.

Phoenix 60p Paperbacks

History/Biography/Travel
The Empire of Rome A.D. 98–190 *Edward Gibbon*
The Prince *Machiavelli*
The Alan Clark Diaries: Thatcher's Fall *Alan Clark*
Churchill: Embattled Hero *Andrew Roberts*
The French Revolution *E.J. Hobsbawm*
Voyage Around the Horn *Joshua Slocum*
The Great Fire of London *Samuel Pepys*
Utopia *Thomas More*
The Holocaust *Paul Johnson*
Tolstoy and History *Isaiah Berlin*

Science and Philosophy
A Guide to Happiness *Epicurus*
Natural Selection *Charles Darwin*
Science, Mind & Cosmos *John Brockman, ed.*
Zarathustra *Friedrich Nietzsche*
God's Utility Function *Richard Dawkins*
Human Origins *Richard Leakey*
Sophie's World: The Greek Philosophers *Jostein Gaarder*
The Rights of Woman *Mary Wollstonecraft*
The Communist Manifesto *Karl Marx & Friedrich Engels*
Birds of Heaven *Ben Okri*

Fiction
Riot at Misri Mandi *Vikram Seth*
The Time Machine *H. G. Wells*
Love in the Night *F. Scott Fitzgerald*

The Murders in the Rue Morgue *Edgar Allan Poe*
The Necklace *Guy de Maupassant*
You Touched Me *D. H. Lawrence*
The Mabinogion *Anon*
Mowgli's Brothers *Rudyard Kipling*
Shancarrig *Maeve Binchy*
A Voyage to Lilliput *Jonathan Swift*

POETRY

Songs of Innocence and Experience *William Blake*
The Eve of Saint Agnes *John Keats*
High Waving Heather *The Brontes*
Sailing to Byzantium *W. B. Yeats*
I Sing the Body Electric *Walt Whitman*
The Ancient Mariner *Samuel Taylor Coleridge*
Intimations of Immortality *William Wordsworth*
Palgrave's Golden Treasury of Love Poems *Francis Palgrave*
Goblin Market *Christina Rossetti*
Fern Hill *Dylan Thomas*

LITERATURE OF PASSION

Don Juan *Lord Byron*
From Bed to Bed *Catullus*
Satyricon *Petronius*
Love Poems *John Donne*
Portrait of a Marriage *Nigel Nicolson*
The Ballad of Reading Gaol *Oscar Wilde*
Love Sonnets *William Shakespeare*
Fanny Hill *John Cleland*
The Sexual Labyrinth (for women) *Alina Reyes*
Close Encounters (for men) *Alina Reyes*